Praise for Dusti Bowling's

SLEUTHING MACHINE!

"A fun series opener with a feisty protagonist who'll keep readers on their toes."—*Kirkus Reviews*

"[Aven Green] is an irrepressible and irresistible narrator, whether reflecting on life as someone born without arms or amicably interacting with her funny friends and family. Unapologetically smart and refreshingly confident in her abilities, this super-sleuth extraordinaire is a joy to tag along with." —*Booklist*

"Aven's candid voice ensures that this chapter book series starter will draw a young audience."—*Publishers Weekly*

★ "Bowling's beloved *Life of a Cactus* protagonist returns in a new series of chapter books that capture her life as third grader. . . . Young readers will laugh aloud at Aven's funny reactions . . . [and] they will be intrigued by the practical skills she has perfected. . . . This chapter book companion to Bowling's well-loved middle grade-series is a recommended purchase."

—*School Library Journal* (starred review)

Aven Green
BAKING MACHINE

By Dusti Bowling

For Younger Readers
AVEN GREEN SLEUTHING MACHINE

AVEN GREEN BAKING MACHINE

AVEN GREEN MUSIC MACHINE

AVEN GREEN SOCCER MACHINE

For Older Readers
INSIGNIFICANT EVENTS IN THE LIFE OF A CACTUS

24 HOURS IN NOWHERE

MOMENTOUS EVENTS IN THE LIFE OF A CACTUS

THE CANYON'S EDGE

ACROSS THE DESERT

Aven Green

BAKING MACHINE

DUSTI BOWLING
illustrated by GINA PERRY

**union
square
kids**

NEW YORK

For Kyle

**union
square
kids**

NEW YORK

UNION SQUARE KIDS and the distinctive Union Square Kids logo are
trademarks of Union Square & Co., LLC.

Union Square & Co., LLC, is a subsidiary of Sterling Publishing Co., Inc.

Text © 2021 Dusti Bowling
Illustrations © 2021 Gina Perry

This paperback edition published in 2022 by Sterling Publishing Co., Inc.

ISBN 978-1-4549-4220-7 (hardcover)
ISBN 978-1-4549-4181-1 (paperback)
ISBN 978-1-4549-4185-9 (e-book)

LCCN number: 2021950664

For information about custom editions, special sales, and premium purchases,
please contact specialsales@unionsquareandco.com.

Printed in Canada

Lot #:
2 4 6 8 10 9 7 5 3

03/23

unionsquareandco.com

Cover and interior design by Jo Obarowski and Shannon Nicole Plunkett

Contents

Chapter 1

Expert Baker Requirements

There are a whole lot of cupcakes, cookies, Rice Krispies Treats, and popcorn balls to make in elementary school. I'm only in the third grade, but I've already become an expert at making these fine foods. And I don't even bake like any old baker. You see, I don't have arms. Yep, you heard me. No arms here on my torso, which I'd like to add is already eight years old.

That means when I crack eggs, I crack them with my feet. And when I measure sugar and flour, I measure them with my feet. And also measuring cups. And when I melt butter, I melt it with my butt cheeks.

Just kidding, of course. I use a microwave like everyone else. Using butt cheeks while baking would be *unsanitary*. Unsanitary is the opposite of sanitary, which means clean. I always wash my feet before I bake, so there's nothing unsanitary about using my feet to bake, and if you try to say so, we might have to have a little talk about how many times you picked your wedgies today using your fingers. Like I said, butt cheeks are unsanitary. It's super hard to pick my wedgies, so I just leave them right there in my butt all day long.

Now, you might be wondering what the requirements are to become an expert baker. The most important thing you need is extra taste buds. Ms. Luna, my third-grade teacher, told us that the average person has about ten thousand taste buds, but I'm pretty sure I have about ten million. I am what is called a *supertaster*. A supertaster is someone whose taste is super.

Something else you need to become an expert baker is a really good sense of smell, so you know when cakes smell delicious and when they smell like poop and are probably inedible. Inedible is the opposite of edible, which just means eatable. I don't know why we don't just say eatable instead of edible, but I imagine someone with a very fancy accent once said eatable like that and a new word was created. Like this one time I said the word "marshmallow" with a very fancy accent like this: *moshmeellowah*. As far as I know, moshmeellowah has not yet replaced marshmallow.

Another thing you need to be an expert baker is buns of steel. Don't worry. I'll explain that later.

But you know what's one thing that's definitely not required for being an expert baker? Having arms. That's what.

Chapter 2

As Many Friends as Possible

I'll never forget the first cake I ever baked all on my own with my mom's help. It was a perfect carrot cake with cream cheese frosting and no nuts because nuts do not belong in cakes or cookies. Anyway, that was last week. Now I'm a pro.

After the carrot cake, I made oatmeal cookies with chocolate chips instead of raisins because raisins taste like sweet mud. Add raisins to the list of foods I will never put into my cookies and cakes. While you're at it, add turnips to the

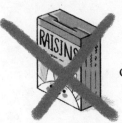

list. Did you know there was such a thing as a turnip cake? I just found out and, people, I am shocked.

The whole reason I've become such an expert baker is because there's a big baking competition coming up at the county fair next weekend and I really, really want one of those beautiful blue first-place ribbons. There's also going to be a live-stock competition, but since I don't have a cow or sheep or chickens and I'm not really sure what a swine even is, I had no choice but to become a professional baker.

In order to win this baking competition, I have decided to enlist the help of my closest friends: Kayla, Emily, and Sujata. I really just became friends with Sujata about a week ago, but you know when you have a special con-nection with someone. Plus, I like to have as many friends as possible at all times. And the wonderful news is that it was Sunday, so they were all coming to my house for an official bakers' meeting. We planned to make one recipe each, which meant four whole baked desserts to "test." Our testing would probably also include eating quite a lot of cookie dough and cake batter. But that's okay because it would be official, scientific testing.

Chapter 3

Milk Barfi

"Someone's at the door," Mom called across the house in a singsongy voice, so I knew it was one of my friends. I ran to the entryway and peeked through the little window next to the door. It was Emily! I smiled and she smiled back. Then she had to wait a few minutes while I unlocked the door with my toes. Sometimes it takes a little longer for me to do things with my toes, and that front door lock was a toughie. Dad keeps saying he's going to replace it with a new one that was easier for me, but that dude is a slowpoke.

Then I called out, "You may enter!" so Emily would just let herself in because that lock had already worn out my toes.

Emily burst through the door, and we jumped up and down excitedly and sang, "Baking day! It's baking day!" and Emily's shrieky voice made my ears hurt a little.

Then Emily put her arm around me, and we ran to the kitchen. She threw her backpack on top of the kitchen table and started pulling out all the cool baking stuff she'd brought: a special chef's hat, an apron, a tiny wooden spoon that came from her doll stuff, a bunch of canned and boxed stuff, a small baking sheet that looked like it could bake about one cookie, and her *sous-chef*, a stuffed dog named Madame Puffy Pants.

A sous-chef is the head chef's assistant. And I was definitely the head chef, so really Madame Puffy Pants was *my* sous-chef.

"What are we going to bake first?" Emily asked all excitedly, just as the doorbell rang. We both squealed and ran to the door. I peeked through the window again and saw Kayla and Sujata standing there.

"You may enter!" I cried, and they came through the door. We all ran to the kitchen, chatting excitedly about the contest.

"We can only enter one dessert in the contest," I told them. "Which means it has to be the very best out of everything we make today."

"Gee, I wonder whose will win," Kayla said, snickering, like she knew exactly whose recipe would win. But, spoiler alert! It wasn't going to be hers.

We stood around the kitchen table, scanning the supplies everyone brought. Kayla had her own chef's hat, a bag of chocolate chips, and pot holders she knitted herself, but instead of being in the shape of squares, they were in the shape of blobs.

We all turned our attention to Sujata's supplies. "What's that?" Emily asked, pointing to a bag of white powder. "Flour?"

Sujata shook her head and smiled shyly. "It's milk powder," she explained.

"We have milk," I said. "You didn't have to bring that."

Sujata's cheeks turned a little pink as she stared down at her milk powder. "My mom thought it might be nice if I brought the ingredients to make a special Indian dessert," she said, running her pink sandal over the kitchen floor and not looking at any of us.

"We weren't sure if you'd have the ingredients, so I brought all of them. And we agreed we could each pick one dessert."

"Great idea!" I announced.

Sujata looked up and smiled.

"Let's make it first!" I said, and Sujata excitedly removed the rest of the ingredients from her backpack, telling us what they were as she did so.

"This is ghee," she explained, pulling out a container.

"What's ghee?" asked Emily

"It's just butter," said Sujata. "But the milk solids have been taken out."

Kayla pointed at the bag of powder. "Are those the milk solids that were taken out?"

Sujata shook her head. "No, that's just milk powder."

We all looked at one another with confused faces. Clearly, none of us had any idea what milk solids and milk powder were. Sujata was really smart.

Sujata pulled out a small tin and opened it. "This is cardamom," she said. "It's a spice." She passed it around for us to smell. Emily stuck her face so far in it that her nose turned brown. I was pretty sure that nose spices were unsanitary, but I didn't say anything.

"That smells superb," I said. "So, what are we making with all this cool stuff?"

Sujata gave us a huge smile. "Milk barfi!"

Again, the three of us looked at one another. Kayla crossed her arms. "Did you just say we're making milk barf?"

Sujata's smile fell. Instantly, she looked down at the floor again. "No, it's called milk barfi. I promise it doesn't taste like barf."

Emily laughed. "We can't make that!"

I started laughing, too. "Who would eat something called milk barf?" I said. "Not me!"

Sujata looked like she might cry, and she ran out of the kitchen. And then I felt like I might cry because our special baking day was not off to a good start.

Chapter 4

Buns of Steel
(I told you I'd explain it)

Mom stormed into the kitchen. "What on earth is going on in here?" she asked. "Why is Sujata in Aven's room crying right now?"

Emily and Kayla and I all looked at one another, and we sure weren't laughing anymore. I shrugged. "Sujata said she wanted to make a dessert called milk barfi, and we said we didn't want to eat it because it sounded like milk barf."

Oh, did mom look mad! She crossed her arms and tapped her foot. "Oh, really? Have you ever *tried* milk barfi before?"

Emily, Kayla, and I sheepishly shook our heads.

Mom nodded. "That's what I thought. Did you ask Sujata what's in it? Or what it actually tastes like? Or why it's important to her?"

"No, we did not ask any of those particular questions," I said.

Emily raised her hand like we were in school. "Oh, oh! There's something called lard bomb in it!"

Mom gave Emily a look that said she had no idea

what Emily was talking about. She sighed and uncrossed her arms. "I want the three of you to go in there right this minute and apologize for being so insensitive. Sujata is your friend, and we don't treat our friends like that, especially when it comes to things we don't understand."

We all three walked into my bedroom. Sujata was sitting on the bed with one of my pillows squeezed to her chest. She wiped at her cheek.

I plopped down next to her. "We're sorry," I said.

Kayla nodded. "Yeah. We shouldn't have laughed about the milk barfi just because it has a funny name. We haven't even tried it yet. We can see how badly we hurt your feelings."

Emily smiled. "Yeah, we won't even know if it actually tastes like barf until we try it," she said, patting Sujata on the back. "And I bet it doesn't even taste like barf at all."

Sujata wiped her eyes. "It doesn't," she said softly. "It tastes like fudge."

"Fudge!" I cried. "Fudge is one of my favorite things in the whole wide world!"

Sujata smiled. "So we can still make it?"

"Let's make it right this very minute!" I declared. So the three of us went back into the kitchen, and Sujata took out the rest of her ingredients.

Since we had to use the stove to make the milk barfi, Mom supervised us. She said she didn't want us to burn the house down.

Sujata melted the ghee butter stuff in a pot, and Emily stirred milk into it. Then Kayla added the milk powder and sugar, and I sat up on the kitchen counter and whisked and whisked and whisked with the whisker in my feet.

I tell you what, whisking with my feet is the best exercise I ever got in my life! Mom has this exercise video, "Buns of Steel," and I thought there was a good chance my buns were turning to steel right there on the kitchen counter.

We sprinkled the cardamom (not lard bomb) in. And then we smooshed it all into a pan with our hands and feet, and Sujata said we had to wait a few hours to eat it, but I could hardly wait. It smelled like spicy heaven and not at all like barf.

Chapter 5

Lots of Refrigerating, No Baking

"My choice next!" I declared. I couldn't wait to tell them what I wanted to make. They would be so impressed. I called Mom back into the kitchen so she could help me do my reveal, just like we rehearsed.

She brought in the big rolled-up poster board. I had drawn a giant picture of my dessert on it. "And now!" I declared, as Mom slowly began to unroll the poster board. "Announcing

the greatest dessert anyone has ever even heard of!" I nodded at Mom because she was unrolling it too slowly. She unrolled the rest and held it up. "Mint chocolate chip pie!"

All three girls clapped, because who wouldn't clap for something called mint chocolate chip pie? People with very bad taste, that's who. And my friends clearly had great taste in desserts, even if they weren't supertasters like me.

While we whipped up the mint chocolate pie filling, I told them, "The baking contest has ten judges who are the best bakers and eaters. One of them even won first place last year with something called a *pandowdy*." And we all laughed, of course, because pandowdy is a hilarious name that sounds kind of like pants-doodie, and who would want to eat pants-doodie?

After we poured all the mint chocolate pie filling into the pie crust, I said, "It has to go into the fridge for a few hours, just like the milk barfi. I hope those judges are wearing an extra pair of socks."

"Why?" asked Sujata.

"Because this dessert is going to knock their socks right off," I declared.

Then we started making Emily's peachy floof, which I thought was the best name for a desert ever. "It's called peachy *fluff*," Emily kept telling us. "I got the idea from a cooking show and made some changes to it so it would be an original Emily dessert."

I was still totally going to call it peachy floof because that was a way better name. And you know what was so funny? It used a lot of the same ingredients as my recipe for mint chocolate chip pie, except it didn't have mint or chocolate or chips or pie in it.

We whipped and *folded* all the peachy floof ingredients together and stuck it in the fridge. "Folding" in this instance just means mixing very slowly and has nothing to do with paper planes or laundry or anything like that.

"Now we have to wait for it to harden up," said Emily.

"I never realized baking took so much refrigeration," I said.

Kayla crossed her arms. "It shouldn't," she said. "We haven't actually baked anything yet."

We all looked at one another. Because Kayla was right.

"When Mom filled out the form to enter the four of us into the contest, the rules said it just had to be an original dessert," I said. "The rules didn't say the dessert had to be baked in an actual oven."

Kayla tapped her foot. "Still, it is a *baking* contest. Don't you think it's time we actually *baked* something?" she said.

"Sure," I said. "Let's bake something instead of sticking it in the fridge!"

Chapter 6

Raisins Ruin Everything

"Let's bake some chocolate chip cookies," I said, walking over to the kitchen table. "We can use those chocolate chips you brought, Kayla." I held the little plastic bag up with my toes.

Kayla laughed. "Those are raisins, Aven! I want to make raisin clafouti." Kayla jutted her chin out. "It's *French*."

I immediately dropped the bag and tried not to gag, so I didn't insult another one of my friends. "Yeah," I said. "We're totally not making that."

Kayla frowned. She crossed her arms. She stomped her foot. "Yes, we are! It's my choice. We all get to choose one thing, right? It's my turn."

"Yeah," I said again. "But see, here's the problem—I'm pretty sure I'm allergic to raisins because they make me choke."

Kayla glared at me. "No one is allergic to raisins," she said.

"I like raisins," said Emily.

"I like them, too," said Sujata. "I've never tried raisin clafouti. I want to try it."

"Well, I don't want to try it!" I declared. "And what's toefooty anyway?"

Mom walked into the kitchen again. "Now what is all the shouting about?"

Kayla told Mom, "I want to make clafouti, and—"

"*Raisin* toefooty," I said, interrupting her.

"Aven said I'm not allowed!" Kayla continued. "And it's clafouti. Not toefooty."

"I never said you weren't allowed," I said. "I just said we totally were never going to make that, not in a million, gazillion years!" I noticed that Sujata had hunched down so low she was nearly hiding under the kitchen table.

Mom looked from me to Kayla and back to me. "I'm so disappointed in your behavior today," Mom said. And can you even believe this? She was looking right at me!

"But Mom," I whined. "Raisins taste like sweet mud. No worse. They taste like sweet diarrhea!"

"How do you know what diarrhea tastes like?" asked Kayla.

"Yeah?" added Emily. "Do you eat it regularly?"

"Yeah," said Kayla. "Are you a diarrhea eater, Aven? Are you a *diarrheater*?"

"No, but you are," I muttered. I could tell I was going to lose this argument.

Mom clapped her hands. "This is absolutely enough," she said. "You're making the raisin clafouti because everyone gets to choose one thing to make, and it's Kayla's turn. Aven has never even tried raisin clafouti."

"And I never will," I said.

"That's just fine," said Mom. "Your loss I'm sure."

"My win I'm sure," I mumbled, so low that no one heard me. "I need to go organize my underwear drawer," I said, stomping out of the kitchen. And guess what? No one was even sad that I left. I could hear them all talking and laughing in the kitchen, including Mom. What a raisin traitor. Mom didn't even like raisins!

I sulked on my bedroom floor, my toes full of underwear. I'd never organized my under- wear drawer before, and I wasn't really sure how to do it—by color?

After a while, the three of them came

into my room. "It's in the oven," said Kayla, just to really rub it in.

I shrugged. "Fine. Whatever," I said.

Sujata spoke up. "Now that we've all gotten to make our recipes, why don't we play stuffy salon?"

"Yes!" said Emily. "Madame Puffy Pants needs to be shampooed. She got some egg on her, and now she's all crusty."

But shampoo just made me think of poo, which is the flavor of raisins. And then I giggled a little because *shampoo* is kind of a funny word.

"What's so funny, Aven?" asked Kayla.

"Shampoo," I said. "Why would they put poo in the name of something you use to make your hair smell good?"

Then the three of them giggled, and I was pretty sure we'd made up. So we played stuffy salon for about an hour, which was good because my stuffed llama, President Ollama, was really stinking up the joint.

Then a smell drifted over all of the shampoo smells, and it wasn't a disgusting smell, much to my dismay. It smelled like something that might even be a little bit delicious.

Then we heard Mom call, "Kayla, your clafouti is done." And the girls all jumped up excitedly and ran to the kitchen.

But I was still not ever going to try that raisin clafouti. *Never ever ever ever never ever!*

Chapter 7

The Final Test

Mom set our desserts out with little plates and forks. They looked lovely all together, except for the disgusting raisin clafouti, of course. That just looked like a round brown thing with those disgusting raisins staring right at me.

First we sampled the milk barfi and, holy moly, was that stuff yummy! "Congratulations, Sujata," I said. "You've made a fabulous dessert."

"This is amazing," said Kayla.

And Emily said something, but her mouth was so stuffed with milk barfi that none of us could even understand what she was saying.

Next we sampled the peachy floof, but I think something went wrong with it because it actually looked like milk barf, for real. "I think peachy *soup* would be a better name for it," I said.

Emily teared up. "I don't know what happened," she said. "Maybe we didn't keep in the fridge long enough."

We all tested it anyway, but we kind of had to drink it. It tasted like sweet fruity cream. "This is

the most delicious sweet fruity cream drink I ever had," I said.

Emily wiped her tears and smiled. "Thank you."

"Yeah, but it's not a drink contest," said Kayla, and Emily's smile fell.

Next we tried the best of all desserts, the sure winner, the mint chocolate chip pie.

Kayla frowned a little. "I think it's too minty," she said.

Sujata chewed. "It's good, though," she said. "I like it."

Emily moved her mouth around all funny. "It's definitely too minty," she said, with her mouth full of cream.

"There's no such thing as too minty," I said, stabbing a bite of that pie with my fork held in my toes and shoving it in my mouth. "It's perfect!" A little bit flew out of my mouth and landed on the table.

"Time for the raisin clafouti!" said Kayla. She dished us out pie-shaped pieces. But I wasn't fooled. This was no pie.

They all dug in, but I just sat there. Those raisins were positively staring at me.

All the girls made noises like it was the most wonderful thing they'd ever tasted. "This is amazing," said Sujata.

"It's so good," said Emily.

"Try it," Kayla said to me.

I shook my head. "I can't. The raisins are staring at me."

"Just pick the raisins out," said Emily.

"But it's all been baked with raisins," I said. "Which means it probably has raisin flavoring."

Kayla rolled her eyes. "Fine," she said. "Your loss."

Yeah, it was my loss. The loss of a mouthful of grossness!

When they were all done stuffing their faces with the evil raisins, Emily broke out our white board, which we usually used for keeping score during our ninja competitions. Then we all voted, and guess what? Not a single one of those stink heads voted for my mint chocolate chip pie, that's what! Emily voted for the milk barfi, and Sujata voted for the raisin clafouti. I voted for the mint chocolate chip pie, of course. Then

Kayla voted for her very own raisin clafouti. I felt kind of bad for Emily because no one voted for the peachy milk soup.

But that meant raisin clafouti won!

"We can't make something I hate for the baking contest," I said.

"You didn't even try it," said Kayla. "So your vote shouldn't count because you didn't try all the desserts."

"My vote should count extra," I said.

"Why?" said Emily.

"Because this is my house and I am the head chef," I said.

"You are not the head chef," said Kayla. "Just acting bossy doesn't make you the boss."

"I'm not bossy," I said. "I order you to take that back right now!"

"You know what," Kayla said with a sly smile. "This is a *baking* contest. And the only thing that *actually* went into the *actual* oven was the *actual* raisin clafouti."

"Yeah, but we still had to cook the other stuff," I said.

"This is not a cooking contest," said Kayla. "It's a baking contest."

Just then there was a knock at the door, and thank goodness it was time for everyone to go home, because I was tired of those girls and their disgusting raisins.

After the girls all left, Mom sat down with me on the couch. "Aven," she said, and I could tell this was going to be real talking-to.

"I know, I know," I said. "You're not appointed in me."

Mom raised an eyebrow. "Appointed in you?"

"Yeah, because you're *disappointed* in me, which must be the opposite of being appointed in me, or that word doesn't even make any sense."

Mom shook her head and rubbed her forehead. "You're right. I *am* disappointed in your behavior."

"Well, I was really disappointed in the raisins," I said, my eyes filling with tears.

Mom sighed. "The Aven I know would try something, even if she didn't want to, so as not to hurt her friends' feelings. You didn't have to eat all of it or even vote for it, but the fact that you wouldn't even try it is upsetting. Kayla was really proud of that clafouti. You did not act like a good friend."

A tear slid down my cheek, and I rubbed it away on the couch cushion. "I'm sorry," I whispered.

Mom put her arm around me. "Don't say sorry to me," she said, and kissed the top of my head. "Say sorry to the friends whose feelings you hurt."

Chapter 8

Kicked Out

The next day at school, all my friends were ignoring me during class whenever I'd try to make eye contact with them. At recess, I saw them all huddled up together near the playground, so I took a deep breath and walked over to them.

They all stopped talking as soon as they saw me coming. "Hi," I said when I got to them.

"Hi," they all said really softly.

"I'm sorry about yesterday," I said.

"That's okay," said Sujata.

Then we all stood there quietly, and I dug my smiley face shoe into the grass. I didn't feel nearly as smiley as my shoes. "So do you want to try out more recipes?" I asked.

"Aven," Kayla said in her take-charge voice. "We're going with raisin clafouti." She looked at the other girls. "And we've decided we don't want you to enter the contest with us anymore."

"But why?" I said, starting to cry again even though I really didn't want to.

"Because you're too difficult," said Emily. "It's your way or nothing."

I looked at Sujata. "Do you think it's my way or nothing?" I asked her.

Sujata looked down at her pink sandals. She didn't say anything, but she didn't need to. I knew she agreed with them but was too nice to say so.

I wiped my cheeks on my shoulder. "Fine," I said. "I don't need you anyway. I'm going to enter by myself and kick all your butts!"

Kayla crossed her arms. "Fine!"

I stomped away and sat on the far side of the art building where no one could see me cry. I didn't need those girls. I could do this all on my own. By myself. With no one's help. Just how I liked it!

Right then, a soccer ball flew by, and Robert came running around the building. "Give me back my soccer ball, Aven Mean Green!" he yelled at me.

It was seriously like a hundred miles from where I was sitting. "I didn't take your stupid soccer ball," I said. "It just rolled over here all by itself." But Robert's words got me thinking. Was I the one being mean? Were my friends right? Was it really my way or nothing?

Robert picked up the soccer ball. He stared down at me. "What's the matter with you?" he asked.

I shrugged. "Nothing. Mind your own business."

Then he sat down next to me. "Did you hurt yourself?" he asked. "Skin a knee or something?"

I pulled my knees up to my chest. "Do my knees look skinned to you?" I said.

"Do you have a bellyache?" he asked.

I shook my head, and I wondered why he was being so nice to me. "I guess I have a little one," I said. I did feel sick—sick about my fight with my friends.

"Do you want to play soccer with us?" Robert asked.

I sniffled and nodded. "Okay," I said.

Then Robert jumped up. "Psych!" he said. "Girls aren't allowed to play because they smell like toads!" Then he ran off.

That guy! I started crying more, and then this other boy from my class, Ren, ran by. I buried my head in my unskinned knees so he wouldn't see me. He stopped anyway and stood over me.

"Are you okay?" Ren asked.

I shook my head. "Just leave me alone," I grumbled.

Instead he sat down by me. Then he patted my back. "Do you need comforting?"

His words made me giggle a little. Then I shook my head. "No, I do not need comforting."

He sighed and dropped his hand. "That's what my mom always says when I'm upset. The comforting usually helps."

I lifted my head. "Okay then. I'll take some comforting."

Ren patted my back again and said, "There, there. Don't worry. It will be okay."

We smiled at each other. "I do feel better," I said. "You're like a comforting expert."

Ren positively glowed. "My mom's really good at it. So what's wrong anyway?"

I told him the whole ugly story, raisiny details and all.

"I don't like raisins either," Ren said.

It was so nice to finally talk to someone who understood. "Do you like to bake?" I asked him.

Ren shook his head. "We don't have an oven at my house, but I do like to make desserts. None of my friends would ever want to enter a contest with me or anything like that, though. They just like sports and video games and stuff like that."

"What's your favorite dessert?" I asked him.

"My mom makes delicious steamed cakes," he said. "That's probably my favorite."

"Steamed cake?" I said, scrunching up my nose and making a funny face.

Ren's smile fell. "They're really good," he said.

"Well, what's in them?" I asked.

"She fills them with this sweet bean paste, and—"

"Whoa!" I interrupted Ren. "She puts beans in cakes? And she steams them?" I scrunched up my nose again and stuck out my tongue, giving him my yuck face.

Ren mumbled, "I hope you feel better soon." And then he walked away all sad.

And I suddenly felt bad about making those faces. I really was Aven Mean Green!

Chapter 9

All on My Own

When I got home from school that day, I told Mom I was going to bake something all on my own. I didn't need anyone to do it with me. I was going to enter that contest by myself and win all by myself and without any disgusting raisin recipes that would just make people gag.

She said that was okay if it was what I really wanted, and she even mopped the kitchen floor so I could do all my mixing down there since it was harder for me to sit on the countertop. Sometimes, when I got on and off the countertop, my clothes caught on the cabinet knobs and tore. And this one time, when I was really little, I got caught on a knob, and I just hung there until someone came and took me off the cabinet! Dad was supposed to change them so they wouldn't tear my clothes, but like I said, he could be a real slowpoke.

She also said she wanted me to let her know before I used anything that could "burn the house down." Why did that lady always think I was going to burn the house down?

I worried about what Kayla said about this being a baking contest and not a cooking contest, so I decided I'd better try making something that had to be baked in the oven. I flipped through Mom's cookbooks until I got to a recipe that looked good: choco-late cake with vanilla frosting. But you know what I figured would make that bad boy even tastier? How about chocolate cake with mint frosting?

I washed my feet, then I took out all the ingredients I needed for the cake: flour (I dropped it and a little spilled all over Mom's clean floor), sugar (I may have also spilled a little), cocoa powder, baking powder, oil, and eggs (I think I may have crushed a few trying to take the carton out of the fridge with my feet).

I placed everything neatly on the floor on top of all the spills and opened the drawer that held the measuring spoons and cups. All of our drawers had good knobs that my toes could handle. I rummaged around with my clean feet.

I saw Mom peek around the kitchen corner. She was spying on me.

Her eyes got all big, too, when she saw the floor. Then she left again.

I carefully followed the recipe as I put all the ingredients into the bowl. So here was the problem, though: it's really hard to lift a measuring cup full of oil without spilling it. And now the oil was sort of mixing with the flour and sugar on the floor and making everything very sticky. I mean, there were toe prints everywhere! If this were a crime scene, I wouldn't even need dusting powder or a magnifying glass to see them.

When the time came to crack the eggs, I did it as carefully as I could with the shells held in my toes. I cracked them right into the cake mix and also smashed egg all over my toes. I put my feet down and peeked in the bowl—there were about fifty billion little shell pieces in there!

I remembered a baking show I once watched. The fancy French chef on there said it was nice to balance something soft with something crunchy, so I figured the eggshells would be okay because of added crunch.

Then I noticed that my eggy toes had gotten in the oily floor goop and they were becoming quite a mess. I washed them again, but it was like trying to wash glue off my feet.

Mom peeked into the kitchen again. "Doing okay?" she asked.

"I'm doing great," I said. "I'm about to bake."

Mom jumped into the room and turned the oven on. Then she looked down at the mess on the floor, but she somehow managed to not say anything about it. Mom really has self-control.

Then Mom helped me put my cake in the oven. While we waited for the cake to bake, we watched our favorite baking show: *Jake's Rake Cake Snake Bake*. Basically, people on the show had to try to bake cakes while snakes slithered around the kitchen, and the only baking tool the contestants were allowed to use was a garden rake, which they also sometimes used to fight the snakes off. It was the best show ever!

Dad got home from work and watched an episode with us. "I really like it when they bring out the anacondas," said Dad.

"I liked it when that woman distracted the snakes with egg bait," I said, and they both agreed with me.

After a little while something started to smell, and let me tell you—it was not a very good smell. Mom pulled the cake out of the oven. It was all flat in the middle and kind of burned on one end.

I mixed up my minty frosting anyway and then I frosted it after it cooled. And now came  the time to test the cake that was going to win the baking contest.

Except it was definitely not going to win the baking contest. Because it was disgusting.

Dad gave me a funny look while he chewed.

"Interesting, Sheebs. What's crunchy in here?"

"Eggshells," I said, and Dad covered his mouth with his hand, but I could still tell he was gagging.

"Honey, did you forget the baking powder?" Mom asked.

Darn it. I did forget the baking powder.

"Is this what you're entering in the baking contest?" Dad asked, forcing down a gulp.

I shook my head. "I can't enter this. It tastes like poop!" Then I ran to my room and cried because I knew I could never win the contest. And my friends were mad at me. And my whole life was a shambles.

Chapter 10

Tomato Soup What???

My friends still weren't talking to me the next day. Or the day after that. I was extra sad when I got home from school, so Mom drove me to visit Great-grandma. Seeing that woman's old face always cheered me up. The first thing Great-grandma said to me when I got there was, "Let's bake something together, Aven."

"Okay, Grandma," I said. "Banana bread?"

Great-grandma shook her head.

"Carrot cake?"

Great-grandma shook her head again.

"What then, Grandma?" I narrowed my eyes at her. "Not . . . turnip cake?"

Great-grandma laughed. "No, Aven. We're going to make tomato soup cake."

I blinked at her because this had to be a big fat joke. "Are you pranking me, Grandma?" I asked.

"Nope," said Great-grandma. "I'm very serious. Let's get started."

I helped Great-grandma put all the usual ingredients for cake into the mixing bowl—flour, sugar, oil, baking soda, baking powder (which I did not forget this time), and eggs. Then Great-grandma pulled out the can of tomato soup.

"You know, Grandma, I think you might want to rethink that tomato soup," I said. "It's not too late to change your mind."

"I'm not changing my mind, honey," she said. Then I watched as she dumped *soup*

into cake. It was a horrendous sight, people. *Horrendous.*

Then Great-grandma popped the cake into the oven. "There," she said. "We'll have delicious tomato soup cake in no time."

Great-grandma and I sat down on the couch together. She put her arm around me. Smitty, her dog, jumped up on the couch with us and put his head in my lap. "You tell your grandma what's the matter," Great-grandma said, patting Smitty's head.

"Grandma," I said, "everyone is mad at me, and they don't want me to do the baking contest with them."

"Why are they mad at you?" asked Great-grandma.

I shrugged. "Just because I didn't want to do the raisin clafouti because raisins are disgusting. And also I guess I made Sujata feel bad when I laughed at the name of her dessert, milk barfi. And also this boy Ren at school told me his mom makes steamed cake with beans in it, and I made a face like this." I showed Great-grandma my yuck face. "I mean, whoever heard of steamed cake with beans in it? That sounds gross."

Great-grandma nodded as she listened to me. When I was finally done explaining the whole situation, she asked me, "Have you ever *tried* steamed cake with beans in it?"

"Of course not," I said.

"So how do you know it's gross if you've never even tried it?" she asked.

"Because beans don't go in dessert," I said. "Whoever heard of sweet beans?"

"You eat my baked beans, and there's lots of sugar in those," she said.

"But that's different," I said.

"How is that different?" she asked.

"You don't put them in cake," I said.

"No, Aven," Great-grandma said sternly. "*You* don't put them in cake. But lots of people around the world use beans in desserts. Lots of people eat all kinds of different things. Even insects."

"I know insects eat all kinds of things, Grandma. They eat mom's tomato plants all day long."

"No, honey," said Great-grandma. "What I meant is that some people even eat insects."

"Gross!" I said.

Great-grandma shook her head. "No, not gross. Just different. If you grew up eating bugs, you wouldn't think it was gross at all. And I bet you eat all kinds of things that some people would think are gross."

"Like what?" I asked.

"Like . . ." Great-grandma thought for a moment. "How about hot dogs?"

"But hot dogs are delicious," I said.

"Some people would think they're gross," she said. "They're made with something that looks like pink slime."

"*Ew*," I said. "But they taste so good."

"And you only know they taste so good because you've tried them, right?"

I shrugged. "I guess so."

"We miss out on all kinds of interesting experiences when we're too scared to try new things," she said.

"Are you saying I should try the steamed cake with beans?" I asked. "But Ren and I really aren't that good of friends. I don't even know if he'd want to give me cake."

Great-grandma sighed. "I'm saying we're all different and have something different to offer this world, Aven," she said. "Even when it comes to cooking and baking. What are you saying when you refuse to try your friends' foods? Or when you make that face?" She copied my yuck face. "Are you saying you're too scared of something that's different? Are you saying it's unacceptable just because it's something you're not used to? What if someone didn't want to eat your food because you made it with your feet? How would that make you feel?"

"Crummy," I said.

"So," said Great-grandma, "How do you think your friends feel when you won't try something, just because it's different from anything you've had before?"

"They probably feel pretty crummy," I said.

Great-grandma nodded. "I bet you're right. The Aven I know wouldn't want anyone to feel crummy, would she?"

I shook my head. "No."

Then the timer went off. "Ah!" said Great-grandma, standing up and causing Smitty to jump off the couch. "Let's see if the tomato soup cake is done."

Great-grandma pulled the cake out of the oven, and I had to admit it smelled pretty good. She stuck a toothpick in it, and it came out clean. Then we whipped up some cream cheese frosting together. "I just don't see how this frosting could taste good on tomato soup," I said.

"True, you may not like it," Great-grandma said, cutting me a square piece of frosted cake and placing it front of me. "But you won't know until you try it."

I took a deep breath, picking up my fork in my toes. I looked down at Smitty sitting next to my chair. "Wish me luck," I told him, but he just drooled. Then I stuck a tiny bite in my mouth. I chewed and chewed, and my eyes got big because, guess what?

Tomato soup cake is delicious!

"It's wonderful, Grandma!" I declared.

Great-grandma nodded. "See how important it is to have an open mind when it comes to trying new things?"

"I totally get it, Grandma! Can I have pickle now?"

"A pickle?" she asked.

"I always have a pickle with my tomato soup. And also grilled cheese, but since the cake has cheese frosting, I guess that will do."

"Well, honey, I really don't think a pickle would go well with tomato soup cake," she said.

"Have you *tried* it, Grandma?"

She smiled. "No, I haven't." Then she got us out two pickles from the fridge. And guess what? Great-grandma's instincts were totally right. Pickles did *not* go well with tomato soup cake. But I could only say that because I tried it.

Chapter 11

A New Partner

At school the next day, my friends were still acting funny around me, and they didn't ask me to play with them at recess again. I would have to figure out a way to make up with them, but first things first.

The fair was only a couple of days away. I walked right up to Ren on the playground, and I asked him if he wanted to enter the baking contest with me.

He shrugged. "I told you I don't even have an oven at home, Aven."

"That's okay!" I declared. "Because I want to try making your mom's steamed cakes that you said are so good. Didn't you say you like making desserts and that you would enter the contest but none of your friends would want to enter with you?"

"I guess," said Ren.

"Well, I'm your friend, right?" I said, and I really hoped he said yes.

He smiled. "Yes," he said.

Phew.

"And I want to enter the baking contest," I said. "Why don't we enter together? And I really want to try those bean cakes."

"Isn't the contest this weekend?" Ren said.

I nodded. "That's why we need to get to work right away!"

"And do you think steamed cake is okay for a baking contest?" he asked.

"The rules don't say anything about the desserts having to be baked in an actual oven." I stared at him. "So what do you think? Do you want to enter with me."

Ren gave me a huge smile and said, "Yes!"

Chapter 12

Manju

Mom drove me to Ren's after school the next day. I really liked Ren's house. His mom made me take my shoes off at the door, which was great because not wearing shoes is always best for me. I mean, how would you feel if you had to wear shoes on your hands all the time? Not very convenient, I tell you.

Ren's kitchen was also really cool, and guess what? It really didn't have an oven! But it had a lot of other neat stuff like fancy rice cookers and a grill right on the countertop and a steamer thingy we were going to use to steam our cakes, which Ren's mom told me were called manju.

Ren and I washed our hands and feet in the kitchen sink, and his mom didn't even have a problem with me sitting on the counter or anything. Then she helped us get out all the ingredients we needed to make the manju— flour, baking powder, sugar, sesame oil, and something called koshian, which is the sweet bean paste.

I gulped at the thought of putting bean paste in the cakes, but I didn't say anything because I hadn't actually tried it yet.

We mixed up all the ingredients except the sesame oil and bean paste. Ren and I kneaded and kneaded that dough with our hands and feet. "I'm getting buns of steel!" I cried, because kneading dough with my feet was really good exercise.

"Oh no," said Ren's mom. "These buns will be very soft. These will not be buns of steel."

I just stared at her because I was pretty sure we were talking about two different buns.

Then we rolled that dough out into little discs and put a glob of bean paste on each one and pinched them up into little sacks. Ren's mom put the little balls into the steamer.

While we waited for the manju to steam, Ren showed me some of his favorite toys—he showed me his cool Lego sets and his cars and his video games. And then he looked at me and he said really seriously, "I feel like I can trust you."

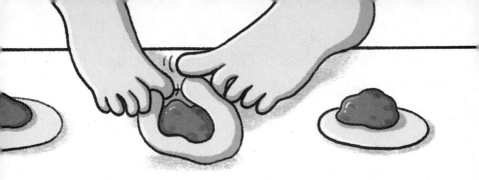

I nodded. "Oh yes, you can. I am as trust-worthy as they come."

Then he went over to the bed and he flipped down the covers and he showed me his abso-lute favorite toy, which was a doll he slept with at night. "My friends would make fun of me if they found out I have a doll," he said.

"I think it's okay for you to like dolls," I said. "I like dolls, too." Ren seemed really happy about that, so we played with his doll until Ren's mom told us the manju were done steaming.

We followed her back into the kitchen, and she scooped them out and put them on plates for us at the kitchen table. I stared at mine.

"Go on," said Ren's mom. "Try it, Aven."

She looked down at me with such sweet, hopeful eyes. I was going to do this. I was going to try cake stuffed with beans. I was!

I took a deep breath, picked up that little steamed cake with my toes, and took a tiny

nibble. I only got a little bit of the beans in my mouth, but you know what? I wanted more!

I took a great big bite, and Ren's mom clapped her hands and laughed. "It's good, isn't it?" she said.

"It's delicious," I said, but my mouth was stuffed so full of manju that I wasn't sure she understood me. But she could definitely tell I loved them.

And that was it—from this moment in history until the end of time, I would forever be Aven Green, trier of new things, even the weirdest things anyone ever heard of. Like—I don't know—like boiled eyeballs. Or fried rattlesnake. Or chocolate-dipped asparagus!

Chapter 13

Aven Is-Sorry-She-Acted-Like-a-Doodie-Head Green

I spent that whole night making cards for my friends. First, I made a thank-you card for Ren and his mom for entering the baking contest with me. I drew a picture of our manju and I glued beans to it. All we had at home were peanuts, but I think it looked really great. I'll never forget the day I found out peanuts were a bean and not an actual nut (mind blown!).

Then I made cards for Kayla, Emily, and Sujata. These were sorry cards because I really was very sorry about everything that had happened. I thought about gluing raisins to the cards, but of course I didn't have any. Instead I used my whole pack of puffy stickers I'd been saving for a special occasion. I'd been saving them for years and years! They had really beautiful butterflies and puppies and kitties on them. I also used my best smelly stickers that smelled like vanilla and chocolate, only the chocolate ones smelled kind of bad. I also used my very best, most expensive glitter glue. I used up the whole tube!

I wrote in big, sparkling letters: *Sorry for being a big stink head!* Then I put the chocolate smelly stickers around it and pointed to them and wrote: *Like these. Because these stink!*

I'm Sorry.

I put all my cards in envelopes, which I would give everyone at the fair.

Robert was wrong—I wasn't Aven Mean Green, even if I'd been acting like it. But I was definitely Aven Knows-When-She's-Wrong Green. Aven Can-Admit-Her-Mistakes Green. And even Aven Is-Sorry-She-Acted-Like-a-Doodie-Head Green.

Chapter 14

The Winner

I went to Ren's house early the morning of the competition so we could make fresh manju. And also play dolls. Then his mom drove us to the fair, where Mom and Dad were already waiting for us.

I guess I'd been expecting everyone working at the fair to clap and get really excited when they saw us coming and say, "We've been waiting for you to begin the competition!" but instead we had to ask several grumpy people wearing STAFF shirts where the baking competition tent was.

We entered the big white tent and saw that it basically just had a lot of folding tables with desserts and little tags all over them. While we were setting out our manju, I saw my three friends walk in with their plates of raisin clafouti. I watched as they set everything up at their table.

I looked up at Mom. She smiled. "Go give them your cards, Aven," she said.

I took a deep breath and walked over to my friends' table. They stopped what they were doing and stared at me. "Hi," I said.

"Hi," they all said.

"I have something for you," I said, motioning with my head down at the little purse I wore across my chest.

Sujata reached inside the purse and pulled out the cards then handed them around. "Thank you," she said.

"You entered the contest with Ren?" asked Kayla.

I smiled. "Yeah. He's really nice."

"I know he is," said Sujata.

"What did you make?" asked Emily.

"We made manju," I said. "It's a steamed bean cake."

Emily scrunched up her nose. "That sounds weird," she said.

"Well, you won't know until you try it," I said. "Anyway, I just wanted to wish you good luck."

Then I walked back to my table. And we waited. And waited. And waited. We waited so long that our fluffy little manju turned all cold and crusty and hard. By the time the judges got around to us, the manju weren't nearly as good as when they were fresh.

Then we all waited while the judges made their decision. And guess what? We totally didn't win first place. But that was okay. I didn't even cry or anything like that.

But guess who did win first place? Some dude I'd never even heard of named Jack Marple with his apple caramel cake. And then some lady named Betty Charles won second place for her chocolate cream pie. And then guess what else?

Emily, Kayla, and Sujata won third place for their raisin clafouti!

When they went up to get their fancy yellow third-place ribbons, you seriously can't believe how loud I cheered for them. I cheered so loudly that Ren's mom looked at me like I was bananas or something. But I was just really happy for my friends.

Then guess what else happened? Those girls walked right over to me and held out one of the yellow ribbons. "Here, Aven," said Kayla.

"They gave us four since we had filled out the form as the four of us."

"We want you to have it," said Sujata.

I looked up at Mom and Dad, and they smiled. I looked at Ren, and he smiled too. But he also still looked a little sad about not winning.

Then I looked back at that beautiful yellow ribbon. It would look so lovely hanging up on my wall next to my best toe painting.

I sighed. "That's really nice of you to offer, but no, thank you," I said.

"You don't want it?" said Emily.

I shrugged. "I didn't win it. Not only that, but I had a bad attitude about the raisin clafouti, which did win."

Kayla put the ribbon down. "Aren't you sad about losing?"

"I didn't lose," I said and smiled at Ren. "I won a whole new friend! And now I have my old friends back, too. Best day ever!"

Then all five of us hugged, and I thought Ren was a great addition to our little group.

We walked over to the award-winning raisin clafouti, and I did something I never thought I would ever do in a million years—I put a little bite in my mouth. And I chewed it up and swallowed it and everything.

"So what do you think?" asked Kayla, her eyes all big and hopeful.

I nodded. "It's for sure an award winner!" I said, and I wasn't even lying. Because it really *was* an award winner, even if I didn't like it at all.

Chapter 15

Music Machine

We all walked through the fair together, and it was so much fun. We visited the livestock competitions, and guess what? I finally found out what a swine is. It's just a pig, which was kind of disappointing. I thought it was going to be some interesting new animal I'd never seen before—like a swan canine. A canine is also just a dog and not even nine of them. Just one dog. English is weird.

We all picked our favorite animals in the livestock tent. Mine was definitely this cute fluffy brown llama. Emily's was this little red poofy chicken called a silkie, which was funny because I also had silky red hair, and I never thought I could ever have anything in common with a chicken. Kayla's favorite animal was a ferocious-looking stallion. Sujata's was a big majestic cow. And Ren's favorite animal was a duck.

When we came out of the livestock tents, I heard some fast drumbeats. "Music!" I cried. "Let's go watch the music!"

We made our way to the big stage area, where a band was playing. "What kind of music is that?" I asked my parents.

"That's bluegrass," said Dad. "It's great, isn't it?"

"I love it!" I cried, shaking my hips and kicking a lot. Because

basically my dancing always amounted to a lot of hip-shaking and kicking. And also maybe some head-bobbing for added spice.

I looked over and saw all four of my friends dancing in a little circle together, and I felt really happy. It had been the best day of all time, and I didn't even win.

"I really love this music!" I yelled at Mom and Dad, who were now dancing together. Dad spun Mom around and they laughed.

"And you're so good at dancing to it," said Mom.

"I'd sure like to be in a band like that," I said. "Then I could make my own music."

"You don't have to be in a band to make your own music," said Mom. "You could learn an instrument if you'd like."

I suddenly stopped dancing and stood there in the middle of the dance floor, breathing hard because dancing is a lot of work. I was having a very big idea. "Do you really think I could learn an instrument?" I asked my parents.

They stopped dancing, too. "Of course we do, Sheebs!" Dad declared.

"We know you can!" added Mom.

And then I kicked so big because I knew it, too! I was going to learn an instrument. "Watch out, world!" I cried. "Here comes Aven Green, Music Machine!"

Aven's Baking Words

Unsanitary: the opposite of sanitary, which means clean. For example, melting butter in a microwave is sanitary, but melting butter with your butt cheeks is unsanitary.

Supertaster: someone whose taste is super (they likely have extra taste buds on their tongue)

Sous-chef: the head chef's assistant

Folding: combining ingredients by carefully and slowly using a spoon to lift the two mixtures together in a bowl, turning them over until smooth; does *not* involve paper planes or laundry

Ghee: butter with the milk solids taken out

Koshian: a smooth, sweet red bean paste made from azuki beans; sometimes called koshi-an or anko

Knead: to prepare dough by pressing, folding, and stretching with your hands or feet

Aven's Recipes

Always make sure to have a
grown-up helping in the kitchen.

Milk Barfi

¼ cup ghee or unsalted butter

¾ cup milk

½ cup sugar

2½ cups powdered milk

¼ teaspoon cardamom powder

¼ cup chopped almonds or pistachios, toasted

1. In a nonstick saucepan, melt the ghee over medium-low heat. If using butter, heat it until it turns a light golden brown and then add the milk, sugar, powdered milk, and cardamom. Whisk until there are no lumps.

2. Cook over medium-low heat, stirring the mixture with a spatula or wooden spoon until it breaks away from the pan (about 10 minutes). Scoop the mixture into a pie pan and smooth down flat. Sprinkle with nuts and press them down. Cover and chill for at least three hours, until hardened.

♦ Mint Chocolate Chip Pie ♦

1 envelope (1 tablespoon) plain gelatin
¼ cup water
2 cups heavy whipping cream, divided
½ cup sugar
1 teaspoon peppermint extract
½ cup mini chocolate chips
1 store-bought chocolate cookie pie crust

1. In a small bowl, sprinkle the gelatin over the water and set aside to soften. Put ½ cup heavy cream in a small saucepan with the sugar and cook over low heat until the sugar has dissolved. Add the peppermint extract and gelatin mixture and stir until dissolved. Set aside to cool to room temperature.

2. Whip the balance of the cream in a stand mixer fitted with the whisk attachment (or with cake beaters) until soft peaks form.

3. Fold the peppermint mixture and chocolate chips into the whipped cream and pour into the pie crust. Chill at least four hours or overnight.

Peachy Floof

1 can (20 oz.) crushed pineapple,
  including juice
1 small package (3 oz.) peach Jell-O
¾ cup sugar
1 package (8 oz.) cream cheese, softened
⅓ cup milk
1 can (15 oz.) peaches, drained
1 cup heavy whipping cream

1. Put pineapple (with juice) in a small
saucepan with the Jell-O and sugar. Simmer
over medium heat until dissolved. Set aside
to cool to room temperature.

2. Whip the cream cheese with the milk
in a stand mixer fitted with the whisk
attachment (or with cake beaters).
Add to the cooled pineapple gelatin
mixture.

3. Mash the canned peaches. Add to the gelatin mixture.

4. Whisk the heavy cream in a stand mixer fitted with the whisk attachment (or with cake beaters) until soft peaks form. Carefully fold into the gelatin mixture. Chill overnight.

Raisin Clafouti

1 tablespoon unsalted butter,
  at room temperature

½ cup plus 1 tablespoon granulated sugar,
  divided

3 extra-large eggs, at room temperature

6 tablespoons all-purpose flour

1½ cups heavy cream

¼ teaspoon salt

1 cup golden raisins (or brown)*

¼ cup powdered sugar

*If you're like Aven, substitute the raisins with 1 cup
 of fruit of your choice: pitted cherries, peeled and
 thinly sliced pears, peeled and thinly sliced apples,
 peeled and sliced peaches, blueberries, raspberries,
 or blackberries.

1. Preheat the oven to 375°F.
   Grease a 9-inch pie pan with
   the butter and sprinkle with
   1 tablespoon of the sugar.

2. Beat the eggs and ½ cup sugar in a stand mixer fitted with the paddle attachment (or in a medium mixing bowl with cake beaters) until light yellow. On low speed, gradually mix in the flour, cream, and salt. Set aside for 10 minutes.

3. Sprinkle the raisins or other fruit into the pie pan. Pour the batter over the fruit and bake for about 35 minutes or until the top is golden brown and the clafouti no longer jiggles when shaken.

4. Sprinkle with the powdered sugar. Slice and serve warm.

Tomato Soup Cake

2 cups flour
1⅓ cups sugar
4 teaspoons baking powder
1 teaspoon baking soda
1 teaspoon cinnamon
1 can (10¾ oz.) tomato soup
½ cup unsalted butter, melted
2 eggs
¼ cup water

Cream Cheese Frosting

1 package (8 oz.) cream cheese,
at room temperature
½ cup unsalted butter, room temperature
2 cups powdered sugar
(note: you may not need all of it)

1. Preheat the oven to 350° F. Grease a
9 x 13-inch baking dish.

2. **To make the cake:** in the bowl of a stand mixer fitted with the paddle attachment (or in a large bowl using cake beaters), mix together all the dry ingredients on low speed. Add the wet ingredients and beat until smooth.

3. Pour into the prepared pan and bake about 30 minutes or until a tester inserted in the center comes out clean. Allow to cool.

4. **To make the frosting:** whisk the cream cheese and butter until light and fluffy in a stand mixer fitted with the whisk attachment (or in a bowl with cake beaters). Add the powdered sugar until the desired sweetness is reached (you don't have to use all of it). Spread on the cooled cake and enjoy!

Manju

VEGAN

1¼ cups flour

3 tablespoons sugar

2 teaspoons baking powder

2 teaspoons vegetable oil

⅓ cup plus 1 tablespoon water

¾ cup koshian smooth red bean paste (may be
purchased at Japanese or Asian grocery stores)

½ teaspoon sesame oil

(NOTE: Recipe requires use of a steamer.)

1. In the bowl of a stand mixer, mix the flour,
sugar, and baking powder. Add the vegetable
oil and water to the bowl and knead for
5 minutes using the dough hook attachment
(if you don't have a stand mixer with a
dough hook attachment, you can mix the
ingredients in a bowl and then knead by
hand or foot on a clean countertop).

2. In a separate bowl, mix together the koshian and sesame oil.

3. Cut the dough into 8 equal pieces and roll into balls. Using a rolling pin, roll each ball into a flat 5-inch disc (if the dough sticks to your surface, sprinkle flour on it to stop the dough from sticking). Place 1 tablespoon of the koshian mixture onto each disc and fold it up like a sack, pinching it together at the top so the koshian is completely enclosed.

4. Place each manju ball on a small square of parchment paper and place into a hot steamer. Steam at medium-high heat for about 10 minutes. Remove carefully with tongs. Enjoy warm!

Author's Note

When I was a child, I was obsessed with reading. Books were one of the most import- ant things in my life, and the authors who created them were my heroes. When I was lonely, books were my friends. They com- forted me when I was upset. And they were there for me when I needed an escape. If one of my favorite authors had ever included me in their creative process, I believe it would have been life-changing. Perhaps I would have even developed the confidence and determination earlier in life to tackle writ- ing as a career. That's why I was so thrilled to involve my readers with this book. Over a hundred people participated in testing Aven's recipes through "Aven's Test Kitchen," and I'm incredibly grateful for their contribution.

And so I hope everyone enjoys both the story and the recipes featured throughout, as Aven grows and learns some meaningful lessons about teamwork, cultural sensitivity, and the importance of being open-minded about trying new things. Happy reading and baking!

Thank you to my test kitchen participants:

Kelly Jo Sadley, Anna Sadley, Jodi Dildy, Ava Dildy, Lucy Dildy, Jessica Barber, Nora Barberger, Suey Lau, Mason Ho, Ava Madrick, Josephine Jones, Cordelia Jones, Shannon Jones, Daniel Drew, Joshua Drew, Jennifer Harris, Addyson Harris, Sophia Smaill, Penelope Smaill, Zoe Smaill, Madeleine Romig, Evelyn Morgan, Daria Taylor, Elly Taylor, Myranda Lefman,

Maxon Lefman, Edward Robinson,
Mandy Priore, Jordan Priore, Eliza Baird,
Olivia Baird, Brad Gustafson, Hope Gustafson,
Christina Strine, Alexis Strine, Jackson Strine,
Wyatt Chadwick, Wendy Chadwick,
Sara Kruger, Lydia Kruger, Leah Howland,
Megan Howland, Molly Place, Avery Place,
Jennifer Starr, Tatum Starr, Jordan Starr,
Lauren Allbright Zutavern, Rowyn Zutavern,
Cate Johnson, Collins McNeeley,
Caroline Guinn, Alex Valerius, Anna Long,
Jacob Davis, Aaron Davis, Jamie Sumner,
Jonas Sumner, Cora Sumner, Luke Gray,
Elise Yu, Ethan Yu, Sue Matthews,
Amelia Matthews, Deena Cook, Grace Cook,
Mae Franzel, Louis Franzel, Ariel Franchak,
Sofia Franchak, Ella Waters, Lyssa Sahadevan,
Turner Sahadevan, Tyler, Rayna Freedman,
Katelyn Stearns, Kinsley Stearns,

Aurea McCullough, Katie Coppens,
Ella Boutis, Luke Boutis, Samantha Boutis,
Aunt Jenny Stebral, Chloe Bee S.,
Lily Dudzic, Niki Shafer, Amaya Shafer,
Grace Gaetano, Alivia Rognstad,
Mya Rognstad, Adele Krenz,
Christina Hanson, Callie Hanson,
Caius Brown, Janet Carson,
Vivian Hope Carson, Halinah Khan,
Farah Khan, Malaika Khan, Bobbie Coccaro,
Sa'Rya Bediako, Emmery Lucas,
Sorelle Taylor, Vivianne Baab, Leia Quach,
Edwin Salazar Turrubiartes, Maika Quashie,
Payton Anderson, Gavin, Kimberly Stewart,
Luke Stewart, Nora Stewart,
Aubrey McAllister, Ainsley McAllister,
Brooklyn Turley, Caitlin Davis, Andrew Davis,
Christopher Davis, Audra Pace, Ethan Pace,
Stori Root, and Cameron Boulton.

Aven Green
can do just
about anything!

She is great
at solving
mysteries in

Aven Green
SLEUTHING MACHINE

She is an
expert baker in

Aven Green
BAKING MACHINE

She is a
professional
musician in
Aven Green
MUSIC MACHINE

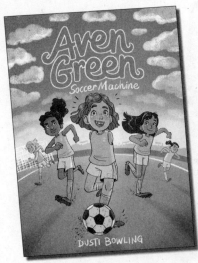

She is a
talented player in
Aven Green
SOCCER MACHINE